Copyright ©2012 by Ronie Powell

All rights reserved.

No part of this book may be reproduced in any form, by Photostat, microfilm, xerography, or any other means, or incorporated into any information retrieval system, electronic or mechanical, without the written permission of the copyright owner.

ISBN-13: 978-1493517725

ISBN-10: 1493517724

The Christmas Healer
© By Ronie Powell

Curly and T. J. reined up on the little rise overlooking the ranch. Neither one said anything for a few minutes – they just pulled their collars up further to ward against the cold and sat looking down on the small spread. Lights were glowing in the windows of the ranch house and bunkhouse, and smoke was coming from the chimneys in both buildings. That Mrs. Duncan; ever since winter had blown in with a vengeance several weeks ago there wasn't a night that they had come in off the range to a cold stove and a dark bunkhouse.

Still not saying anything, each lost in their own thoughts, they eased their mounts off the ridge and down the hill to headquarters. Curly and T. J. were hands for the "R J" – the only hands. "The Roscoe John Cattle Co." – a big name for a small ranch with a few hundred head of mother cows. John Duncan, the owner, had included his good cow horse Roscoe when naming the outfit as a young single cowboy. "After all", he always said, "If it weren't for him and the part he played in the early days there wouldn't be a cattle company". John always was one to give credit where credit was due. Yep, he sure had been a good boss. He expected no more from you than he was willing to give himself, and he knew the importance of a word of praise or a pat on the back when it was needed. Shoot, Curly and T.J. would have followed him off a cliff if he'd asked them, and there was no doubt that Mrs. Duncan and those two little boys thought he'd hung the moon. That's what made things so gosh-darned hard now, and the reason Curly and T.J. were so silent. John had been killed a month ago.

Ever true to the code of extending your hand to your neighbor, he had ridden out on a brisk fall morning to help the neighboring outfit gather strays from their summer range before the first snows hit. Leaving Roscoe to rest, as they had finished the long drive that took their own cattle to their winter range a few days before, he chose instead a green colt that needed some hours and miles.

From the way they read the sign when they found him the next day, he must have been flat out down a slope after a cow when his colt landed wrong and went end over end, crushing John underneath him as he rolled. Although he was still alive when they brought him in, pneumonia had already set in from his night on the mountain. It's hard to say whether it was that or the colt rolling on him that killed him. The cause of his death didn't much matter, it was the fact that he was gone that had sure made this a pretty sorry outfit ever since.

Financially, Mary and the boys were all right. The calves had been shipped before John's accident, the bills had been paid for the year, and with plenty of snow in the mountains already they were pretty well assured of enough run-off for good grazing in the spring. After twelve years of working side by side, Mary knew as much about the business end of the operation as John had. By calculating what they had used in prior years she knew they had enough hay put up to see them through the worst of winters, and they had developed such a good market for their calves that she wasn't worried about finding buyers when next fall rolled around. For what she might not know about the cattle, Mary knew that she could count on Curly and T. J. The problem was that John's death had so devastated Mary and the boys that their spirits were broken. Instead of the great love she had once felt for the ranch, she just felt numb inside, and John Jr. and Matt were hollow-eyed shadows of their former selves.

Mary looked at the boys as they sat listless in front of the fire. John Jr., 10, and the image of his dad with red hair and green eyes, and Matt, 6, with dark curly hair and doe eyes like herself, sat quietly as they had each night since their crying stopped. Like her, they were lost without John, and to top it off, tomorrow night was Christmas Eve. Christmas had always been a special holiday at the ranch, filled with laughter, song, and merriment, but without John there to share it, it would be meaningless.

Mary was especially worried about John Jr. Matt was still young enough that Mary was the most important thing in his life. John Jr., however, had idolized his father, and when he lost him it was as it he had lost part of himself. She looked at both boys, lost in their own thoughts, and spoke. "Boys, are you sure you wouldn't like a Christmas tree? I can still have Curly or T.J. cut one for us."

Matt looked up hopefully, but John quickly spoke up. "No Mama, it just doesn't seem like Christmas without Daddy here." And with that he turned back to the fire.

'Perhaps she should have pushed the issue', Mary thought to herself, but her heart wasn't in it either, and she was just as happy to forego Christmas altogether. As she turned her attention back to the stove where supper was cooking, she glanced out the window to see Curly and T. J. riding into the corral.

Curly, who in reality was bald, had been with John and Mary since they married 12 years ago. A gruff and taciturn west Texan, somewhere past 50, Curly knew what a cow was thinking before she did. His oversized hands and enormous frame held a heart as big as all outdoors, and his size was matched only by his loyalty. Curly had never said much about his life before coming to the ranch, but Mary had always sensed a sadness deep within him, and only John had known that it was due to the death of his wife and son during childbirth. He had sold his own little spread in west Texas and come to Colorado seeking to escape the painful memories that greeted him everywhere he turned. John and Mary didn't really need any help in the early days, but John had seen something in Curly that made him extend his hand and welcome Curly as a valued member of the outfit. Time had dulled and eased Curly's pain to the point where it became bearable, but John's death had re-honed the edges of his own grief and added its sharp sting to the grief he felt at the loss of his good friend. All of this went through Curly's mind as he unsaddled and tended to his horse before going into the ranch house for supper.

T. J. was watching Curly rub his horse down as he went about his own chores, wishing he could share his feelings of loss over John's death, but not knowing how to start. A gangly and awkward youth, barely past his teens, he was like a sack full of clumsy until you put him on a horse. Mounted, with a rope in his hand, he became poetry in motion. An orphan, kicked from foster home to foster home as a kid, he had come to the ranch four years ago and found a home. John and Mary and the boys had been the best thing that ever happened to him. Even Curly had been a steadfast and true friend, and a teacher. But now he felt an ache inside far beyond what he had ever felt at being an orphan; after all, he'd never known his parents. Before he could think how to start, Curly had finished with his horse and said, "C'mon kid lets go to supper".

The two men started to the ranch house just as Mary was stepping out the back door to ring the dinner bell. With only two hands, meals had always been served in the main house – besides, Mary and John had always thought of Curly and T. J. as part of the family. In the past, meal times had always been lively gatherings with the buzz of the day's events, news from town or other outfits, and a healthy dose of play and kidding between T. J. and the boys. Since John's death, however, all of that had changed. These days an awkward silence reigned. Each member of this once happy group was so busy trying to deal with their own feelings that no one knew what to say to each other. Except for some brief small talk about the day's work, and plans for the following day, most of which Mary now left up to Curly, not much was said.

As the men finished their meal, thanked Mary, and stood up to leave, she spoke up. "Curly; T. J., you know tomorrow is Christmas Eve. The boys and I have decided not to celebrate Christmas this year, but I want you to take tomorrow afternoon and Christmas day off as usual. If you'd like to go to town please feel free to take the truck –

the boys and I can handle things here." Curly and T. J. glanced at each other and then Curly replied, "Thank you ma'am, but I need to work on my saddle and T. J.'s bay gelding needs shoeing, so I think we'll just stick around here."

"All right then," she replied, and then added, "We've been fattening that turkey for Christmas anyway, so I'll at least make us a special Christmas Eve supper tomorrow night."

When Curly and T. J. got to the bunkhouse not much was said for awhile until
T. J. could stand it no longer and finally blurted out, "Shoot Curly, I know that Mrs. Duncan and them kids are grieving, and I am too, but heck, it's still Christmas, and them kids deserve to have some sort of a Christmas. I went through enough years without Christmas as a kid to know that much."

Curly didn't say anything for a few minutes and T. J. began to wonder if he'd heard him, but then he nodded, as if to himself and said, "Kid, you're right, and you've made me realize something." And with that they began to talk and make their plans for the following day.

Christmas Eve morning saw Curly and T. J. each ride off in a different direction, and it wasn't until nearly supper time that Mary looked out and noticed that they were back and busy with something in the barn. Feeling that the occasion called for it even if she didn't feel like being festive, she put on a good dress and fastened the cameo brooch that John had given her on their wedding day onto the collar, and then stepped out to ring the dinner bell.

Mary had just finished putting the food on the table when Curly and T. J. came in. After everyone was seated and the blessing had been given, Curly spoke up.

"Ma'am, if you don't mind, there's something I'd like to say before we start. We've been a pretty sorry bunch around here since we lost John. We've all been lost without him and we've kept our grief to ourselves, and if you'll forgive me saying so ma'am, we've been wrong. The way you handle grief is to share it, and the way you get past it is to remember the good times that you had. John taught me that."

Curly could see that Mary looked pained, but he pressed on. "Ma'am, we can't stop living just because John isn't here to live life with us. And I hope you won't think we're out of line, but me and T. J. don't think that he would want your or these boys not to celebrate Christmas just because he's gone, so we've got something for each of you."

T. J. stepped to the back door and came back in with a furry bundle in his arms. "Matt" he said, "this pup is for you. Your daddy was telling me not long ago that it was about time you had a dog of your own, and seeing as the Simmons' good heeler had pups – well, here he is".

Matt hugged the pup tight and looked up with a smile amidst his tears as he said "Thank You!" Then he buried his face in the pup's soft fur and whispered quietly "you and me are going to be best friends."

Then Curly pulled a small item that was wrapped in a bandana out of his pocket and handed it to John Jr. "Son", he said as the boy opened it to reveal a small Case knife with his dad's initials on the nameplate, "your dad gave me this several years ago when I lost my knife, and the last time we talked he told me that you had lost yours, so I think this rightly belongs to you." Before anyone could say anything, Curly continued, "And ma'am, there's a two-year-old filly in the barn out of old man Porter's good King bred mare. John bought her for you this summer as your Christmas gift and Mr. Porter's been keeping her for you all this time. I rode over today and brought her home."

For a few minutes no one spoke, and then Mary quietly began to cry and Curly was afraid they'd really botched things. But through her tears she looked up and smiled and said, "Thank you Curly. You're right – we can't stop living, and I'm afraid that's just what we've done." And then she began to talk, about John and about all of the wonderful times they had shared. And one by one, each of them except John Jr. joined in with memories of special times that they had shared with John and what he'd meant to them. A lot of tears were shed that night, but there were a lot of smiles and laughter too. And four people who had been trapped inside themselves by their feelings slowly felt the pain of their loss melt away as they shared it with each other.

Mary was still concerned, however, about John Jr. He had spent the whole time just turning that knife over and over in his hand. When the meal was finished he finally spoke up.

"Mama, I know that Daddy always took a basket of things to Mr. Porter on Christmas Day. If you will get it ready, and Curly and T. J. will help me catch and saddle Roscoe, I'd like to take it to him." No one said anything for a minute, but then Mary and Curly and T. J. each looked at each other and smiled, and each one thought to themselves that perhaps they hadn't totally lost John after all.

A Farmhouse Christmas

© By Ronie Powell

It was Friday, December 23, 1932 and a snowstorm was raging outside the rambling white farmhouse on Oak Hill. It was fine to be inside by the wood stove on such a day, but Fred couldn't help but be disappointed as the steadily falling snow meant no Friday trip to town to barter milk, eggs and ham for supplies, and thus no chance to enjoy the sights and sounds of town and perhaps come home with a piece of candy tucked away inside his coat. And it definitely meant no heading to the woods with his rifle for a day of hunting, a pass time that he loved better than anything else.

His Grandfather Cornish had given Fred his first rifle and taught him to shoot at 10 years old, and by the age of 11 Fred was spending every moment that he could in the woods. It was not uncommon for him to leave the house before daybreak with only a sandwich and an apple, and perhaps one of his grandmother's molasses cookies if he was lucky, and to return well after dark. By now, at 14, this handsome young man with auburn hair, a determined jaw, and sharp intelligent eyes knew every tree and plant, and the habits of all of the woodland creatures. And whether he came home with a pheasant, partridge, or a rabbit or two tucked in his coat, or came home with berries, watercress, bittersweet, or wild pears that he gathered in his travels, every day spent in the woods was the best of days. But, with the storm raging outside there would be none of that today, and the thought of spending the day shut up in the house was almost unbearable.

***

Morning chores had been completed at the crack of dawn as usual with Grandfather Cornish and his father, Leon, leading the way to the barn while Fred brought up the rear. Down with a bout of bronchitis, Fred's 12-year old brother, Mike, was still tucked in bed when the three men, for Fred already thought of himself as a man, started out.

Snow was falling at a steady pace and already piling up when they'd entered the barn, but inside was cozy with the sweet smell of hay and the comforting smells and sounds of the milk cows and work horses. Fred didn't particularly like milking, but he did enjoy the animals, particularly the two dappled gray work horses, Kit and Fan, and he spent some time rubbing on and talking to them in response to their nickers as he filled their mangers with hay and brought them to the trough for a drink, while his dad and grandfather did the milking. The horses put him in such good humor that Fred didn't even mind tending to the hogs and chickens, though he usually thought of those chores as 'child's work' and delegated them to his brother whenever possible.

As they made their way back to the farmhouse for breakfast the wind picked up considerably and two older men realized that they were in for a real Nor'easter.

Grandfather Cornish had hoped to be able to make it to town that day to trade and barter for some Christmas gifts for the family, at least for the boys, but that was not going to happen and the thought of not having anything for the children was like a bitter pill.

'Well', he thought, 'the depression has been hard on everyone and we're luckier than most as we have plenty of food and wood and a good roof over our heads.' Still, he knew it was going to be a pretty glum Christmas. But as they gathered as a family around the big kitchen table for breakfast, he gave a hearty blessing and beamed at his sweet-faced wife and his tall and slender daughter, Marie. As was typical in that era, the Drake farm in upstate New York was home not only to Leon and Marie and their two boys, but to Marie's parents, Carrie May & Frederick, as well. And as was also typical, breakfast on a working farm was a hearty meal served after morning chores were done, and designed to keep working men and women well fueled until dinner at mid-day. This morning they all sat down to thick slices of ham they had cured themselves, mountains of pancakes with fresh maple syrup produced from the sap from their own trees, a big skillet of fried potatoes and a huge pot of coffee. And even though the storm was raging outside there was fellowship and good cheer around the kitchen table.

But now, with breakfast over and few prospects for entertainment available, Fred lingered by the wood stove in the front parlor anxious for something to pass the time. He knew better than to disturb his father who sat at the desk deep in thought with a ledger in front of him. A slender and raw boned man with a serious nature and little humor, Leon has lost his mother in a tragic accident at only 5 years old and had been farmed out to work for his living at 9. His life had been filled with hard work, hard times and little affection, and though he loved his wife and sons it was rare to see him laugh or smile, and he kept his words sparse, and his emotions close to the vest.

With his mother and grandmother busy at work in the kitchen preparing food for the rest of the day, Fred knew better than to make an appearance there looking for entertainment because he would likely be given 'kitchen chores', and he dreaded that even worse than milking. Instead he decided to hunt up his grandfather to see if he might be coaxed into a game of checkers or chess.

Fred's grandparents had a large and sunny bedroom right off the kitchen, and though Fred adored both of them, it was with his grandfather that he had the most special of bonds. A well educated and thoughtful man with a wonderful and wicked sense of humor, Frederick adored his grandsons and delighted in spending time with them and sharing not only his wisdom, but his philosophy on life and how to live it. His handsome face and twinkling blue eyes reflected his love of life and family, and when Fred came wandering in to the bedroom his quick smile indicated he was more than happy to put down the book he'd been reading and move to the parlor for a game of checkers. After all, not only did it present an opportunity for some lively competition, it gave him an audience for his insightful and witty commentary on all subjects.

***

After filling the morning and part of the afternoon playing checkers the men headed to the barn earlier than usual for the afternoon chores. The snow and the wind had kept up their assault all day and by late afternoon the drifting snow and howling winds made the trip to the barn an effort, and despite their layers of clothing, the bite of the wind and cold quickly took a toll on fingers, toes and cheeks. Extra rations and bedding were distributed to all of the creatures that made their home on the Drake farm, for the family were good stewards to their livestock and to their land. Even King, their farm shepherd, was allowed to come in from the wood shed to the warmth of the kitchen when they finally made their way back to the house, and he politely curled himself away in a corner near the wood stove and promptly went to sleep.

As the family gathered around the table for supper, young Mike now feeling a bit better and able to join them, Leon spoke up; "This storm shows no signs of stopping. With the Depression and the weather I think we should just be thankful for what we have and forget about celebrating Christmas this year."

Looking around the table Fred saw his mother and grandmother with downcast eyes and sad expressions, and saw his grandfather's mouth firm into a straight line. Sneaking a look at his brother, he saw two tears well up in the corner of the blonde-haired boy's blue eyes, and felt his chest fill with a combination of disappointment and bitterness. He hadn't expected presents. He knew what the depression had meant for the family. And on his trips to town he had seen other families in much worse shape than his own, so he was grateful for their warm and cozy house and for the bounty of food they had stored away. Still, he had hoped for a tree and some sort of special celebration, for Christmas had always been a special and magical time on the Drake farm and the prospects of not even recognizing Christmas left him with a hollow and empty feeling.

Fred's grandparents shut themselves away in their bedroom right after supper was cleared away, and with his mother busy tending to Mike and his dad lost in thought with a serious expression at his desk, Fred decided to just call it a day and went to bed early.

Very little heat made its way from the woodstoves downstairs to the upstairs bedrooms, so shucking his clothes as quickly as possible and jumping into the bed in his long underwear, Fred burrowed down under the multitude of quilts that his mother had piled on his bed and waited for warmth and sleep to come and he soon drifted off to dreams of slipping through the woods in pursuit of a whitetail buck.

***

In their bedroom off the kitchen, Carrie May and Frederick were deep in conversation. Deeply respecting that their son-in-law was the head of the household, they were still concerned and saddened by his decision to forego any sort of Christmas celebration. After talking for awhile, Carrie May turned in for the night, but Frederick sat for a while longer, deep in thought, and then arose and made his way to the woodshed. After letting King out for a quick run, they both returned to the warmth of the kitchen and Frederick got to work.

***

Daybreak on Christmas Eve found the wind dying down and the snow beginning to slow, but the 24 hour storm had taken its toll and the farm on Oak Hill was buried under more than 2 feet of snow. The men struggled to the barn to do the morning chores and were more than happy to return to the warmth of the house for breakfast. Fred noticed that his mother and grandmother seemed particularly cheerful in spite of his father's declaration that they would not be celebrating Christmas and he couldn't help but notice how often they had their heads together in whispered conversations and wondered to himself what they were talking about.

After feasting on bacon and eggs accompanied by large slices of toasted home made bread topped with home made preserves, steaming bowls of oatmeal and fresh coffee, Frederick excused himself and headed for the back door.

"Where are you going Granddad? Can I go with you?" Fred asked.

"No son", he replied. "This is a chore for me alone. I won't be gone long. You tend to the fires and help your mother and grandmother if they need anything". And with that he disappeared out the back door.

Quickly deciding that retreat from the kitchen was wise unless he wished to be stuck there helping the women, Fred soon found himself settled down in the parlor with a Zane Grey novel. As avid a reader as his grandfather, Fred spent several hours buried in his book until his nose and stomach started telling him that there were some delicious odors emanating from the kitchen, and with a start he realized that his grandfather had not yet returned. Rushing to the kitchen to ask where granddad was, Fred was greeted by the order to 'wash up for lunch' and 'don't worry about your grandfather.'

As the family gathered around the table for steaming bowls of hearty beef and vegetable soup and a pan of golden corn bread (or 'Johnny cake' as his grandmother liked to call it) fresh from the oven, Fred couldn't help but notice that his grandmother and mother seemed worried that his grandfather was still gone, although they were doing their best not to show it. Mike ate quietly, still not completely recovered from his bronchitis, and Leon still seemed lost in his own thoughts and not overly concerned with Frederick's absence. When Fred tried to express his concerns, he was quickly hushed up by his mother, and when he asked what they'd been baking that smelled so good he was told they'd been baking for a neighbor who was under the weather and to mind his own business. Frustrated, but realizing that argument was futile, he again retreated to the parlor and his book to pass the time until evening chores.

A short time later he heard the stamping of feet in the kitchen and a hearty, "Daughter! Get me some coffee and a bowl of that soup! It's cold enough to freeze your whiskers out there!" Rushing to the kitchen Fred was relieved to see that his grandfather had returned safely, but when he tried to question him about where he'd been and what he'd been doing the subject was quickly changed, and after lunch Granddad once again retreated to his room and shut the door.

When the evening chores had been finished and the men had returned to the farmhouse for supper, Granddad gave the blessing as usual and then held up his hand for silence. Turning to Leon, he spoke;

"Son, I know that you expressed the desire to not celebrate Christmas this year, and I respect that, but I just felt the need for a Christmas tree to commemorate the event. I went out this afternoon and cut down a beautiful little spruce I've had my eye on all year, and it's out by the wood shed. Would you help me make a stand for it and get it in the house after supper, and perhaps the boys could string some popcorn and make some paper chains to decorate it?"

Everyone held their breath waiting for Leon to speak. Silent for awhile, he eventually nodded his head and said, "Sure Frederick, I'd be happy to help you with it". And with that it felt as though a black cloud that had hung over the family had been whisked away. Suddenly there was cheerful talk and laughter around the table, as plans were made for how they might decorate the tree. Kitchen chores were done in a flash with everyone pitching in as Frederick and Leon made a stand for the beautiful little spruce. And while they were getting it set up the boys busied themselves making decorations. Paper chains were glued together, batches of popcorn were popped – some for Carrie May's famous popcorn balls, and some for stringing, and Marie helped the boys shape a beautiful star for the top of the tree from bits of tin foil she had saved.

When the tree had been decorated to everyone's satisfaction, and the boy's stomachs were full of Carrie May's sweet and sticky popcorn balls, Frederick gathered the family about him as he read the story of Christ's birth from the gospel of Luke. Even Leon got up from his desk and came to sit with the family, and when the reading was finished he spoke up;

"Marie, I wonder if you and your mother would consider making something special for our Christmas dinner tomorrow? We're certainly blessed with food if nothing else. And perhaps we could take something to our neighbor, Mr. Rumsey. He's been under the weather with bronchitis as well and it would be good to check on him."

"Of course dear", Marie replied. "We'd be happy to, wouldn't we mother."

And no one seemed to notice the little wink that the women exchanged with each other. Only Frederick knew that they'd spent much of that day, at his suggestion, preparing favorite dishes that were traditional to their Christmas celebration. Even now there were mincemeat and pumpkin pies and molasses cookies tucked away in the pie safe, and a turkey being brined to go into the oven in the morning. It would be accompanied by Marie's famous stuffing, a mountain of mashed potatoes with gravy, roasted and candied sweet potatoes, green beans they had canned themselves, cranberry sauce cooked fresh from their store of dried cranberries gathered from a local bog, and of course home made yeast rolls with freshly churned butter and strawberry preserves the women had cooked and canned last spring.

Everyone retired to bed with much lighter hearts that Christmas Eve, but Frederick soon slipped back into the kitchen to complete his task and it was several more hours before he finally nodded with satisfaction at his completed work and slipped into bed.

Christmas morning dawned bright and snapping cold. The storm had finally ended during the night and now the family awoke to a glorious winter wonderland. The sun was almost blinding in its brilliance, but it revealed one of nature's most glorious sights; the beautiful rolling farmland completely blanketed in pristine white snow. Hills and valleys, forests and fields, stone fences and wooden ones, barns and houses were all draped in white fluff.

Fred made his way to the kitchen, and to the warmth of the wood stove, pulling on clothing as he went. He couldn't wait to get outside and make the first tracks through the unmarked blanket of white. But before he could head out the door his grandfather stepped from his bedroom and stopped him. As Leon and Mike entered the kitchen granddad spoke up.

"Son", he said to Leon; "I know you asked us to forget about celebrating Christmas this year, and I respect that. But I hope you'll forgive Carrie May and me if we've overstepped any bounds." And with that he led the family into the parlor.

There, under the tree, were thick wool socks that Carrie May had knit for Leon and the boys, and a beautiful knit cap and scarf she had made for Marie. But what caught Fred's eye was a hand carved Tin Lizzie and a hand carved horse just the image of Kit. As he gazed at them he felt Mike grab hold of his arm and they both looked up at Granddad with wide eyes. As he twinkled back at them he said,

"Now boys, your grandmother spent considerable time knitting those fine socks for you. I know you're excited about them, so go ahead, you can put them on."

"But Granddad…" Mike began. But before he could finish Fred piped up, "Granddad, are these for us?"

"What's that?" Frederick asked. "Oh, this Tin Lizzie? Well, I know Mike loves automobiles and I thought he might like a replica of ours, just to remember it by. And I know you've got quite a fondness for old Kit, so I thought you might like a replica of her." And with that the boys flew into his arms.

And as Frederick looked up Leon very quietly said, "Thank you Dad. Merry Christmas everyone". ©

Made in the USA
Charleston, SC
12 December 2013